The Lost Island

Published in 2004 by Simply Read Books Inc.
Cataloguing in Publication Data

Johnson, E. Pauline (Emily Pauline), 1861-1913
  The lost island / Pauline Johnson ; illustrated by Atanas Matsoureff. - 1st ed.
  ISBN 1-894965-07-8
  I. Matsoureff, Atanas II. Title.
PS8469.O283L67 2004   C813'.4   C2004-900029-2

Illustrations copyright © 2004 Atanas Matsoureff

10 9 8 7 6 5 4 3 2 1

Designed by Roberto Bruzzese, www.robertobruzzese.com
Printed and bound in Italy by Grafiche AZ

The Lost Island

E. Pauline Johnson

Illustrated by Atanas

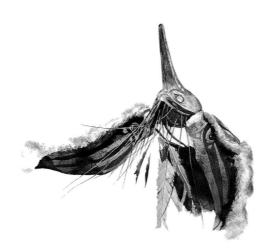

Simply Read Books

"Yes," said my old tillicum, "we Indians have lost many things. We have lost our lands, our forests, our game, our fish; we have lost our ancient religion, our ancient dress; some of the younger people have even lost their fathers' language and the legends and traditions of their ancestors. We cannot call those old things back to us; they will never come up again.

"We may travel many days up the mountain-trails, and look in the silent places for them. They are not there. We may paddle many moons on the sea, but our canoes will never enter the channel that leads to the yesterdays of the Indian people. These things are lost, just like 'The Island of the North Arm.' They may be somewhere near by, but no one can ever find them."

"But there are many islands up the North Arm," I asserted.

"Not the island we Indian people have sought for many tens of summers," he replied sorrowfully.

"Was it ever there?" I questioned.

"Yes, it was there," he said. "My grandsires and my great-grandsires saw it; but that was long ago. My father never saw it, though he spent many days in many years searching, always searching for it. I am an old man myself, and I have never seen it, though from my youth, I, too, have searched. Sometimes in the stillness of the nights I have paddled up in my canoe." Then, lowering his voice: "Twice I have seen its shadow: high rocky shores, reaching as high as the tree-tops on the mainland, then tall pines and firs on its summit like a king's crown. As I paddled up the Arm one summer night, long ago, the shadow of these rocks and firs fell across my canoe, across my face, and across the waters beyond. I turned rapidly to look. There was no island there, nothing but a wide stretch of waters on both sides of me, and the moon almost directly overhead.

"Don't say it was the shore that shadowed me," he hastened, catching my thought. "The moon was above me; my canoe scarce made a shadow on the still waters. No, it was not the shore."

"Why do you search for it?" I lamented, thinking of the old dreams in my own life whose realization I have never attained.

"There is something on that island that I want. I shall look for it until I die, for it is there," he affirmed. There was a long silence between us after that. I had learned to love silences when with my old tillicum, for they always led to a legend. After a time, he began voluntarily.

"It was more than one hundred years ago. This great city of Vancouver was but the dream of the Sagalie Tyee at that time. The dream had not yet come to the white man; only one great Indian medicine-man knew that some day a great camp for Pale-faces would lie between False Creek and the Inlet. This dream haunted him; it came to him night and day – when he was amid his people laughing and feasting, or when he was alone in the forest chanting his strange songs, beating his hollow drum, or shaking his wooden witch-rattle to gain more power to cure the sick and the dying of his tribe. For years, this dream followed him. He grew to be an old, old man, yet always he could hear voices, strong and loud, as when they first spoke to him in his youth, and they would say: 'Between the two narrow strips of salt water the white man will camp, many hundreds of them, many thousands of them. The Indians will learn their ways, will live as they do, will become as they are. There will be no more great war-dances, no more fights with other powerful tribes; it will be as if the Indians had lost all bravery, all courage, all confidence.'

"He hated the voices, he hated the dream; but all his power, all his big medicine, could not drive them away. He was the strongest man on all the North Pacific Coast. He was mighty and very tall, and his muscles were as those of Leloo, the timber-wolf, when he is strongest to kill his prey.

"He could go for many days without food; he could fight the largest mountain-lion; he could overthrow the fiercest grizzly bear; he could paddle against the wildest winds and ride the highest waves. He could meet his enemies and kill whole tribes single-handed. His strength, his courage, his power, his bravery, were those of a giant. He knew no fear; nothing in the earth or the sky could conquer him. He was fearless, fearless. Only this haunting dream of the coming white man's camp he could not drive away; it was the only thing in his life he had tried to kill and failed.

"It drove him from the feasting, drove him from the pleasant lodges, the fires, the dancing, the story-telling of his people in their camp by the water's edge, where the salmon thronged and the deer came down to drink of the mountain-streams. He left the Indian village, chanting his wild songs as he went.

"Up through the mighty forests he climbed, through the trailless deep mosses and matted vines, up to the summit of what the white men call Grouse Mountain.

"For many days, he camped there. He ate no food, he drank no water, but sat and sang his medicine-songs through the dark hours and through the day. Before him – far beneath his feet – lay the narrow strip of land between the two salt waters.

"The Sagalie Tyee gave him the power to see far into the future.

"He looked across a hundred years, just as he looked across what you call the Inlet, and he saw mighty lodges built close together, hundreds and thousands of them – lodges of stone and wood, and long straight trails to divide them.

"He saw these trails thronging with Pale-faces; he heard the sound of the white man's paddle-dip on the waters, for it is not silent like the Indian's; he saw the white man's trading posts, saw the fishing-nets, heard his speech. Then the vision faded as gradually as it came. The narrow strip of land was his own forest once more.

" 'I am old,' he called, in his sorrow and his trouble for his people. I am old, O Sagalie Tyee! Soon I shall die and go to the Happy Hunting Grounds of my fathers. Let not my strength die with me. Keep living for all time my courage, my bravery, my fearlessness. Keep them for my people that they may be strong enough to endure the white man's rule. Keep my strength living for them; hide it so that the Pale-face may never find or see it.'

"Then he came down from the summit of Grouse Mountain. Still chanting his medicine-songs, he entered his canoe and paddled through the colours of the setting sun far up the North Arm.

"When night fell, he came to an island with misty shores of great grey rock; on its summit tall pines and firs encircled like a king's crown. As he neared it, he felt all his strength, his courage, his fearlessness leaving him; he could see these things drift from him on to the island. They were as the clouds that rest on the mountains, grey-white and half-transparent. Weak as a woman, he paddled back to the Indian village; he told them to go and search for 'The Island,' where they would find all his courage, his fearlessness and his strength, living, living for ever.

"He slept then, but—in the morning, he did not awake. Since then our young men and our old have searched for 'The Island.' It is there somewhere, up some lost channel, but we cannot find it. When we do, we will get back all the courage and bravery we had before the white man came, for the great medicine man said those things never die —they live for one's children and grandchildren."

His voice ceased. My whole heart went out to him in his longing for the lost island.
I thought of all the splendid courage I knew him to possess, so made answer : "But
you say that the shadow of this island has fallen upon you; is it not so, tillicum?"

"Yes," he said half mournfully. "But only the shadow."

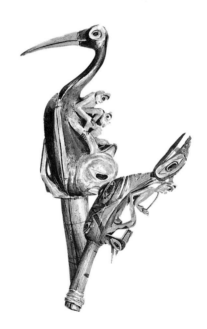